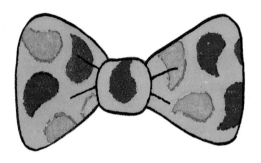

For
Eileen

First published 1992 by Walker Books Ltd
87 Vauxhall Walk, London SE11 5HJ

This edition published 2007

2 4 6 8 10 9 7 5 3 1

This book has been typeset in AT Arta.

Printed in China

British Library Cataloguing in Publication Data:
a catalogue record for this book is
available from the British Library.

ISBN 978-1-4063-0993-5

www.walkerbooks.co.uk

Monday Run-day

Nick Sharratt

WALKER BOOKS
AND SUBSIDIARIES
LONDON · BOSTON · SYDNEY · AUCKLAND

Monday
run-day

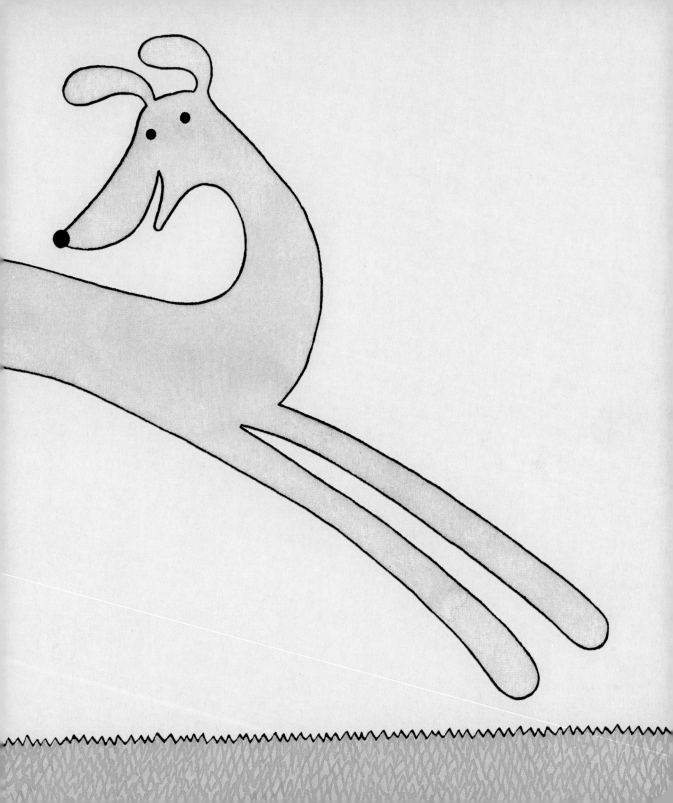

Tuesday
snooze-day

Wednesday
friends-day

Thursday
grrrs-day

Friday
tie-day

Saturday
splatter-
day

Sunday
bun-day

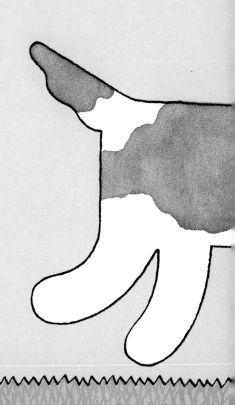

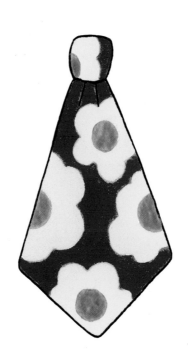